Winkie-The Cross Eyed Witch

Verse By
Mildred McDowell

INTRODUCTION

Winkie — The Cross Eyed Witch, another in the series of story and verse texts published by Unicorn Enterprises, enables your child to conclude that witches are not always frightful beings. Winkie in fact is not frightful at all. She does not even possess extreme magical powers; however, she continually causes disruption. Winkie has a very bad habit — she cannot remember to wear her glasses. Therefore, a series of blundering, comical events results in this "oversight." The weatherman and the other witches suffer most from her chaotic forgetfulness. Yes, even witches have problems, but Winkie does redeem herself at the conclusion of this "bewitching" story. This is evidenced in the first two lines of the last stanza of the poem which follows the story.

"When Winkie and Biddy landed,
 The cheering was heard far and near."

The latter quote exemplifies how completely the story is summarized within the verse. This technique of fusing Story and Verse into one text is a means of engendering high interest and motivation within the child.

The child is also exposed to a vocabularly building process. For example, the reader will note that with the addition of such suffixes as *ly* and *ing* new word forms are developed from familiar words that the child has previously implemented. All in all *Winkie — The Cross Eyed Witch* serves not only to entertain, but educate.

Sandra L. Harman
Reading Consultant
Teacher of English
Cincinnati Public Schools

"Winkie" The Cross Eyed Witch

By
Bridget Fitzgerald

Illustrations
Fran Kreger

STORY AND ITS VERSE BOOKS

Printed and Published in U.S.A. by
UNICORN ENTERPRISES, CINCINNATI, OHIO

INTERNATIONAL STANDARD BOOK
NUMBER 0-87884-020-6

LIBRARY OF CONGRESS CATALOG CARD
NUMBER 71-189878

The Story

Winkie never remembered to wear the glasses the witch doctor gave her. So, she began to fly her broom into her aunts', cousins', and sisters' brooms sending favorite cats sailing into the air, screeching and crying. Winkie would always beg their pardon, and fly off singing. Meanwhile the witch she bumped into would grumble and set her hat back on her head.

The weather man did not like to
see Winkie fly by. If he said there
would be rain, sure enough she
would fly away with the rain cloud
trailing on her broom.

If the weather man said that there would be a clear, sunny day, Winkie would come back from a trip and pull a large cloud over the sun's face.

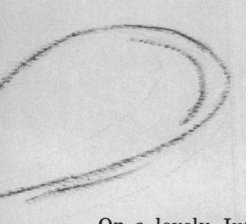

On a lovely June morning, Winkie
wanted to visit Aunt Kate. Aunt Kate
lived on the other side of the mountains. Winkie was up bright and early
and so was her cat, Biddy. Off they
sailed on a new broom. New brooms
are often hard to fly, and Winkie's was
very hard today.

Winkie flew low so that she could see
the beautiful gardens, the tiny houses
and the river. Suddenly the broom shot
straight up in the air, and it was all
Winkie could do to stop before she
reached the moon.

When she came down through the
clouds, she was lost. Where was she?
Where were the beautiful gardens, the
river and the tiny houses that the
witches built deep in the woods. Where,
oh where, were the mountains? Poor
Winkie flew on and on.

At last she saw the river! Holding the broom tightly — down she zoomed. Splash! The broom took Winkie and Biddy into the water.

Winkie was ready to scream, but she and her cat just shook themselves off, got back on the broom, and flew toward home. They would go to Aunt Kate's another day on their old broom.

Back at home, the witches made their special brew. They started as soon as Winkie was not around to bother them. First one witch and then another would run to the large oak tree. Some carried the big black pot — while others brought red, blue, yellow and green bottles.

Everyone worked very fast and very hard. No one even stopped for lunch. Just before it was time to pour the brew into the bottles — the pot caught fire! You know the one thing witches fear most is fire. If one teeny, tiny spark touches them, they go up in smoke and are gone forever.

While the other witches were running every way and into each other — WINKIE APPEARED IN THE SKY. As down she flew, she saw smoke, but could not see anyone! She heard screams and cries. She flew lower to see what was happening.

hurrah !!

HURRAH WINKIE!

Hurrah!!

HURRAH !!!

Hurrah
for w

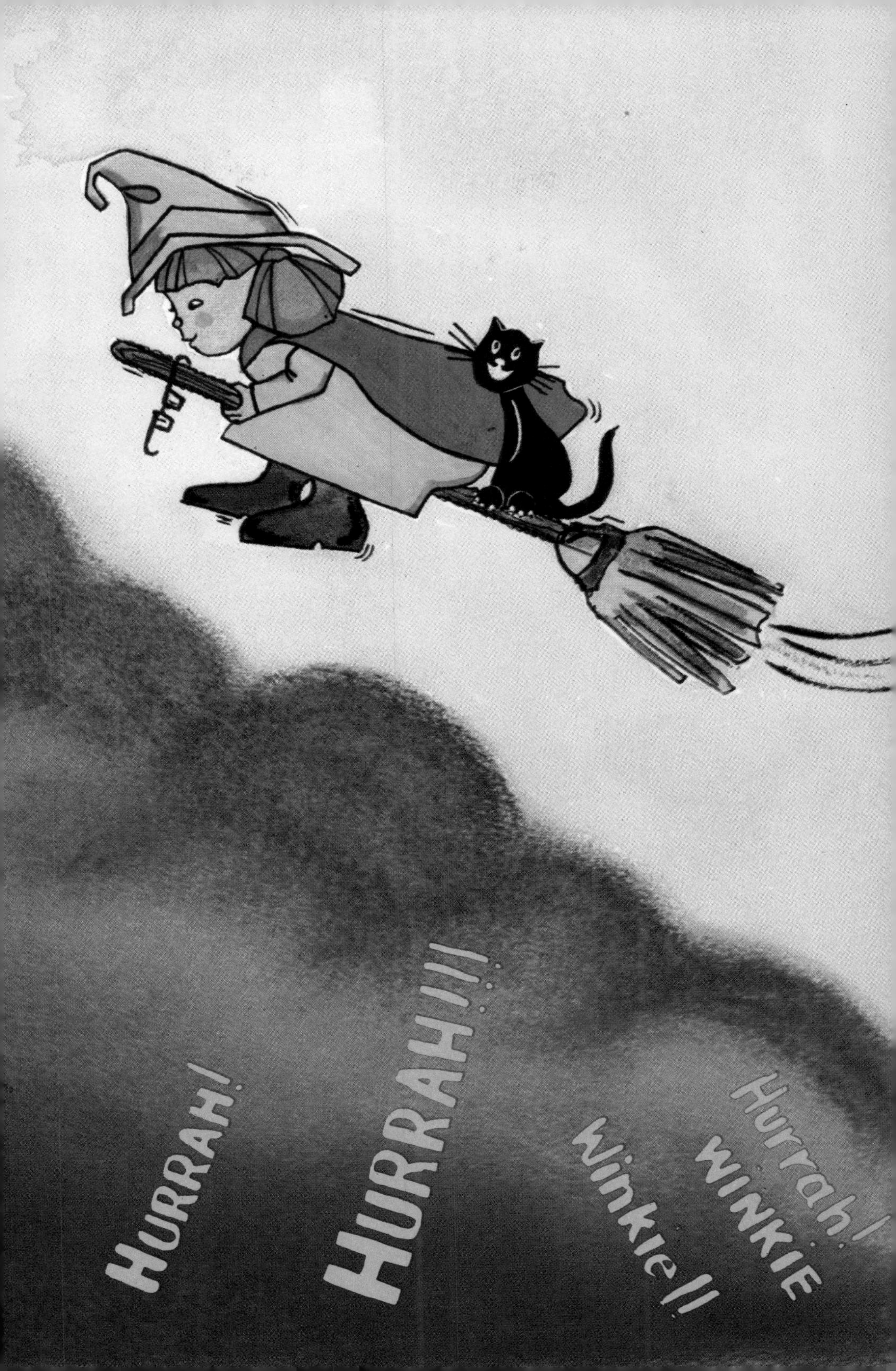
HURRAH!
HURRAH!!!!
Hurrah!
WINKIE
Winkie!!

Suddenly she heard loud shouts, "HURRAH FOR WINKIE!" "HURRAH FOR WINKIE!" Winkie was so surprised that she stood up on her broom and turned around. She could not see the fire. All she could see was a large rain cloud that she had pulled down from the sky. The witches were running around bumping into each other. Now their voices were gay and happy because the fire was out.

Winkie and Biddy landed on the ground. All the witches gathered around to meet them. Every face was dirty, smiling and happy.

After that, not one witch ever spoke when Winkie bumped into them or knocked their favorite cat in the air, though every witch secretly wished Winkie would wear her glasses.

The Verse

Her glasses were very important,
    The witch doctor told her so.
But Winkie could never remember,
She had so many things to do.
She would bump into other witches,
Scaring their cats in her flight.
She would pull down big black clouds,
Changing day into night.

She went to visit Aunt Kate,
Taking Biddy along for the ride.
The new broom was hard to handle,
She came down in the river wide.

When the witches got rid of Winkie,
They started to cook up a brew.
They didn't know how the fire started,
They didn't know what to do.

Coming back with a rain cloud behind her,
Winkie heard loud shouts below.
She waited a few more minutes,
And then came down real slow.

When Winkie and Biddy landed,
The cheering was heard far and near.
The fire was out, the danger passed,
The witches had nothing to fear.